oops
this
is
a
smurglet

this
is
a
smurglet

TO &
WESTON &
SIERRA —
Have fun finding
all the sandburglers
in the Birthday bird
 — Susan
12/3/10

Smurglets are Everywhere

Poems by Alan Birkelbach

Illustrations by Susan J. Halbower

TCU Press
Fort Worth, Texas

Poems copyright © 2010 by Alan Birkelbach
Illustrations copyright © 2010 by Susan J. Halbower

Library of Congress Cataloging-in-Publication Data

Birkelbach, Alan.
 Smurglets are everywhere: poems/by Alan Birkelbach; illustrations by Susan J. Halbower.
    p. cm.
  ISBN 978-0-87565-415-7 (alk. paper)
 1. Children's poetry, American. I. Halbower, Susan J., ill. II. Title.
 PS3552.I7543S68 2010
 811'.54--dc22
                          2010001503
TCU Press
P. O. Box 298300
Fort Worth, Texas 76129
817.257.7822
http://www.prs.tcu.edu

To order books: 800.826.8911

Designed by Bill Brammer at fusion29
Printed in China by Everbest through Four Colour Imports, Ltd., Louisville, Kentucky

Acknowledgments: Poetry Society of Texas Book of the Year 1981, Poetry Society of Texas for "Where the Dwermies Dwell"

To Laura, the kids, and especially the grandkids

–Alan Birkelbach

For Will, Tom and David

–Susan J. Halbower

About the Author

Alan Birklebach has been writing poetry since he was twelve years old. In fact, his first poem ever was about his pet raccoon!

Photo courtesy of the University of North Texas

Since then he has written thousands of poems. He writes mostly about Texas, its towns, its history, and its geography. His work has appeared in journals and anthologies such as *Grasslands Review, Borderlands, The Langdon Review,* and *Concho River Review.* He has received a Fellowship Grant from the Writer's League of Texas, been named as one of the Distinguished Poets of Dallas, was nominated for a Wrangler Award for his contributions to Southwest Letters, and is a member of The Academy of American Poets. He has five collections of poetry: *Bone Song, Weighed in the Balances, No Boundaries, New and Selected Works* (the first in the TCU Texas Poet Laureate Series from TCU Press), and *Translating the Prairie: Plano, Texas in Words and Pictures.*

In 2005 Mr. Birkelbach was named the poet laureate of Texas.

About the Illustrator

Susan J. Halbower has a degree in art from Kenyon College, but she learned to watercolor making books for her three young nephews. From that came a line of cards and stationery, bow wow CARDS, and various design commissions ranging from t-shirts to invitations.

Photo courtesy of Mallory Samson

She was delighted to have the opportunity to illustrate Alan Birkelbach's vivid poems, and thanks the many smurglets who guided her in this project, and continue to surprise her.

The Poems

Ogres Hate Okra

They're Everywhere!

Whole Lotta Shakin'

What's on the Menu

Maybe I Should Watch Penguins

Giant Robot on the Loose!

The Edge of the Earth

Ride the Burro Instead

Tyrannosaurs Make Pizza

Weldon Wing, the Armpit King

But It Was Such a Deal!

Shall We Meet Again at Lunch?

Anaconda Cargo

I Prefer the Combo

Brok the Thunderrer

I've Lost My Blue Galoopa

My Plan for Success

One Missing Ingredient

The Elephant

Caveman Frozen in the Ice!

Unfair Comparison

Leading the Way

When Blob Jr. Went to Camp

Tom Pterodactyl

Medusa and Her Sister

The Exhausted Woodpecker

Camping on Skull Island

Lizard Trouble

Potatoes Are Attacking

Sleepover!

Sylvia Snorkleby

Where the Dwermies Dwell

Finale

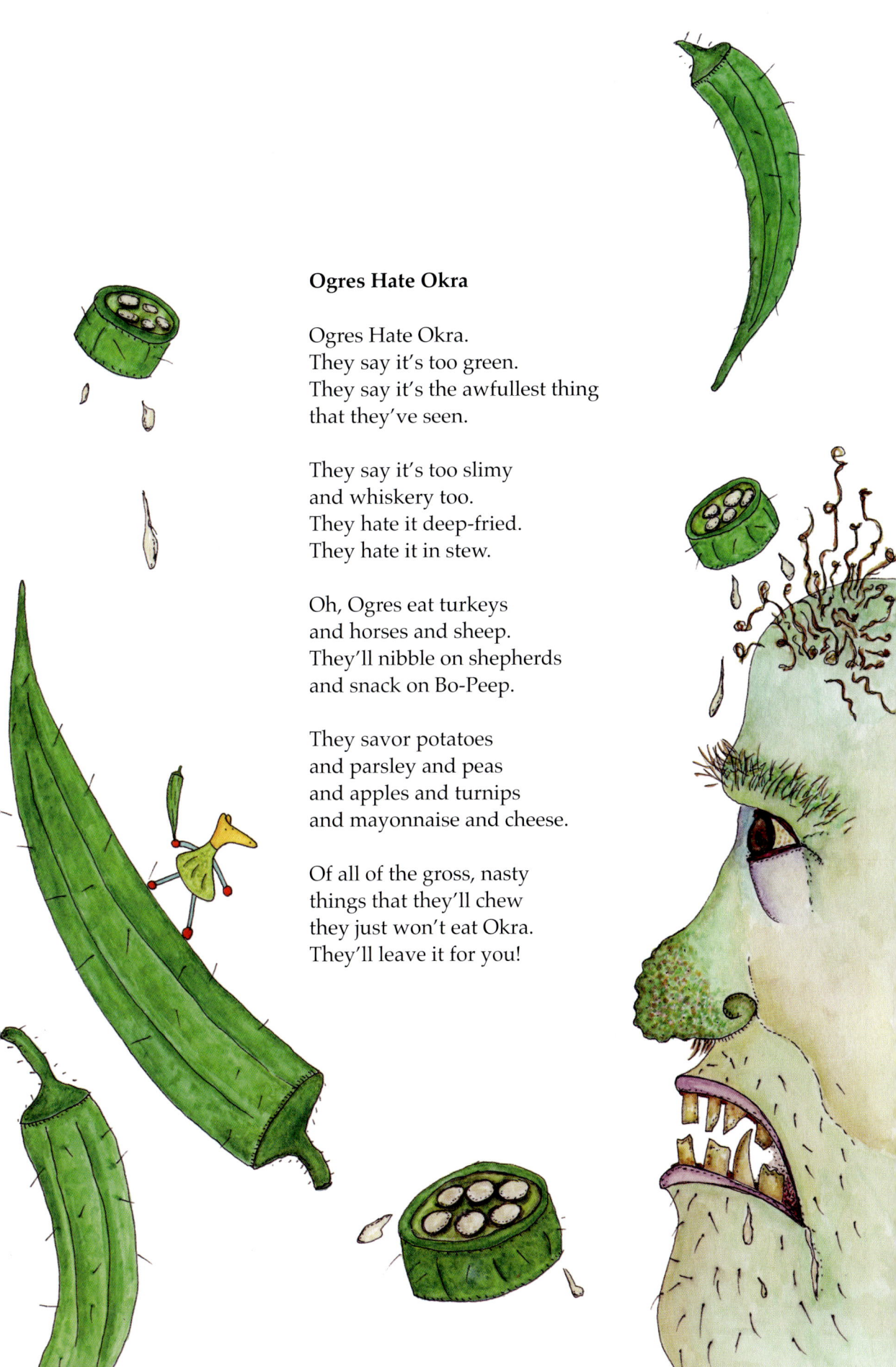

Ogres Hate Okra

Ogres Hate Okra.
They say it's too green.
They say it's the awfullest thing
that they've seen.

They say it's too slimy
and whiskery too.
They hate it deep-fried.
They hate it in stew.

Oh, Ogres eat turkeys
and horses and sheep.
They'll nibble on shepherds
and snack on Bo-Peep.

They savor potatoes
and parsley and peas
and apples and turnips
and mayonnaise and cheese.

Of all of the gross, nasty
things that they'll chew
they just won't eat Okra.
They'll leave it for you!

They're Everywhere!

Mr. Bibbles, rare inventor,
built a smurg madigulator
and it generated smurglets
on a fanduloso scale.

There were smurglets bright and twirmy.
Some were tall and some were swirmy.
Some were spotted, some were flappled,
and some even had a tail.

Mr. Bibbles, in elation,
took an overjoyed vacation
for his smurg madigulator was
a bambulous success.

But he left the darn thing running.
It kept running, running, running,
and it kept on making smurglets
which is why we're in this mess.

They saw they were unshackled.
They smooted and they brackled.
They frew and trew, and smackled
on their little dippled feets.

The smurglets kept on coming
'til the very walls were humming,
and they grabbled through the doorways,
and they poured into the streets.

Now there's smurglets doing taxes,
painting houses, getting waxes.
They are drippling from the gutters.
They are coming out the hose.

There are smurglets in the sockets,
deep in everybody's pockets,
and that's why there are smurglets
bathing in your fruity-o's.

Whole Lotta Shakin'

When you drive through Wiggleburg
do like the natives do.
Drop into the diner
and have a shake—or two.

You must wiggle as you order
from your head down to your feet.
You must wiggle as you swallow peas
and as you chew your meat.

You must wiggle, wiggle, wiggle,
wiggle, wiggle in your booth.
You must wiggle as you eat dessert.
It's expected! That's the truth.

The waitress will be wiggling
and the busboy and the cook!
(The tourists who aren't wiggling
all get a wiggly look.)

Please wiggle as you pay the bill.
Please wiggle as you go.
Until you pass the city limits
wiggle to and fro.

And then just when you think that you
can now be calm and still,
the little town just down the road
is known as Giggleville.

What's on the Menu

The wicked witch's house next door
was made of gingerbread.
Since people don't eat sweets as much
she used lunch meat instead.

The chimney's made of corned beef.
The sidewalk's made of ham.
The shingles are baloney
and the garden gnomes are Spam.

The bricks are liverwurst and veal.
The hose is stringy cheese.
The garden tools are gouda.
Those are pepperoni trees.

The fountain's on a schedule
so you might have to wait.
It shoots out mayonnaise 'til four
and mustard, four to eight.

Oh sure, the house is magic,
and looks like lots of fun,
but lunch meat doesn't hold up good
when left out in the sun.

I wish that witch would switch her plan
and cast another spell.
Oh please go back to gingerbread!
It sure would help the smell!

Maybe I Should Watch Penguins

I take my cues from Nature.
It's how I learn the best.
Just yesterday I watched
a mother robin in her nest.

I heard, "Cheep, cheep! More Insects, Please!"
That mother would take flight.
Her baby birds all seemed to have
an endless appetite.

I quickly learned it takes a lot
of bugs to fill a beak.
I paid real close attention
to the nurturing technique.

My sister's in her high chair now.
Just look at how she squirms.
She's not too fond of crickets
so I'm moving on to worms.

Giant Robot on the Loose!

My Giant Robot just got out.
I didn't lock the door.
Could you help me catch him?
It's happened twice before.

He's only eighty-four feet tall.
He'll leave a trail behind.
He's not too good at hiding.
He won't be hard to find.

He's probably down at the mall
so there's no need to rush.
He claims the escalator flirts—
and now he has a crush!

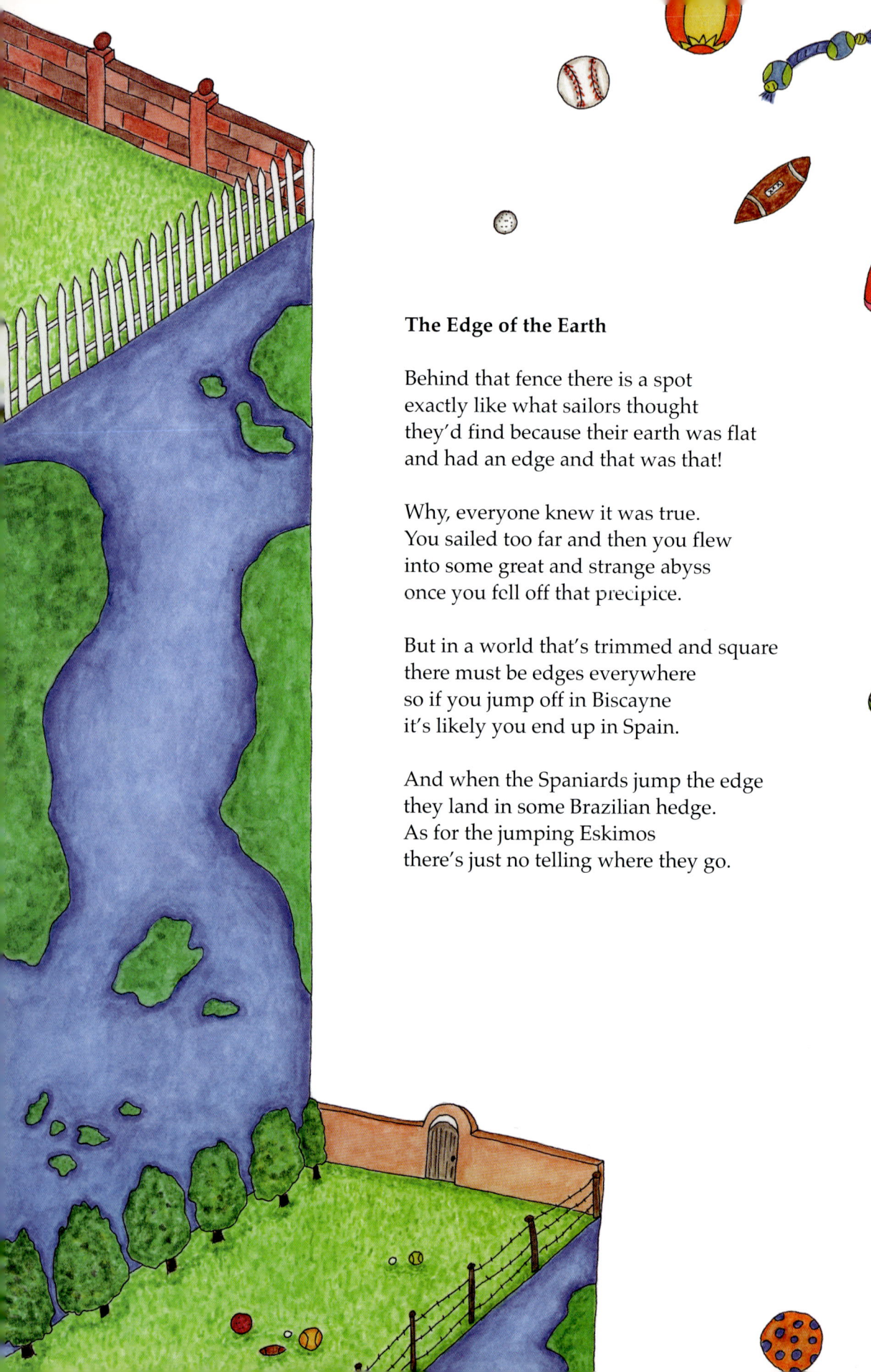

The Edge of the Earth

Behind that fence there is a spot
exactly like what sailors thought
they'd find because their earth was flat
and had an edge and that was that!

Why, everyone knew it was true.
You sailed too far and then you flew
into some great and strange abyss
once you fell off that precipice.

But in a world that's trimmed and square
there must be edges everywhere
so if you jump off in Biscayne
it's likely you end up in Spain.

And when the Spaniards jump the edge
they land in some Brazilian hedge.
As for the jumping Eskimos
there's just no telling where they go.

But like I said, behind that fence
is some strange kind of turbulence.
I've lost a dozen balls or more.
They sail across—and are no more!

Footballs, kick-balls, horse-shoes, hats—
I don't where know my stuff is at!
I peek as soon as they take flight—
Where do they go? They're not in sight!

And now I have to go tell Dad
I think that I did something bad.
To find the last ball that I lost
I threw my brother right across.

No way I can avoid Dad-jail.
My brother sent us in the mail
a letter saying, "Don't be long.
I have your ball. I'm in Hong Kong."

Ride the Burro Instead

If you try to ride the Bongo
you won't stay on very longo.
He will head off to the Congo
and bounce you off like pingo-pongo.

Tyrannosaurs Make Pizza

Tyrannosaurs make pizza.
How can that be so?
Their little arms are perfect
for making pizza dough.

Their little arms can make a pizza sauce
that's sure to please.
They chop the pepperoni.
They even grate the cheese.

Tyrannosaurs use their small arms
to lay this out with grace.
And then they use their big back legs
to stomp it all in place!

Weldon Wing, the Armpit King

Weldon Wing, the Armpit King,
could really make his armpit sing.
His underarm had such a toot
you'd want to stand up and salute.

Birthdays, weddings, foreign guests—
He played for them—and did requests!
He's ambi-pits-trous so you'd see
him use both hands for harmony.

Something tender for your mom?
He'll squeeze one out with such aplomb
that it will make your mother sigh
and dab at something in her eye.

He went and had a CD made
to play for friends in second grade:
a treasury of greatest hits
which he entitled "It's the Pits."

Whatever the event demands
he's got the perfect pits and hands.
Bar mitzvahs, banquets—anything!
Call Weldon Wing, the Armpit King!

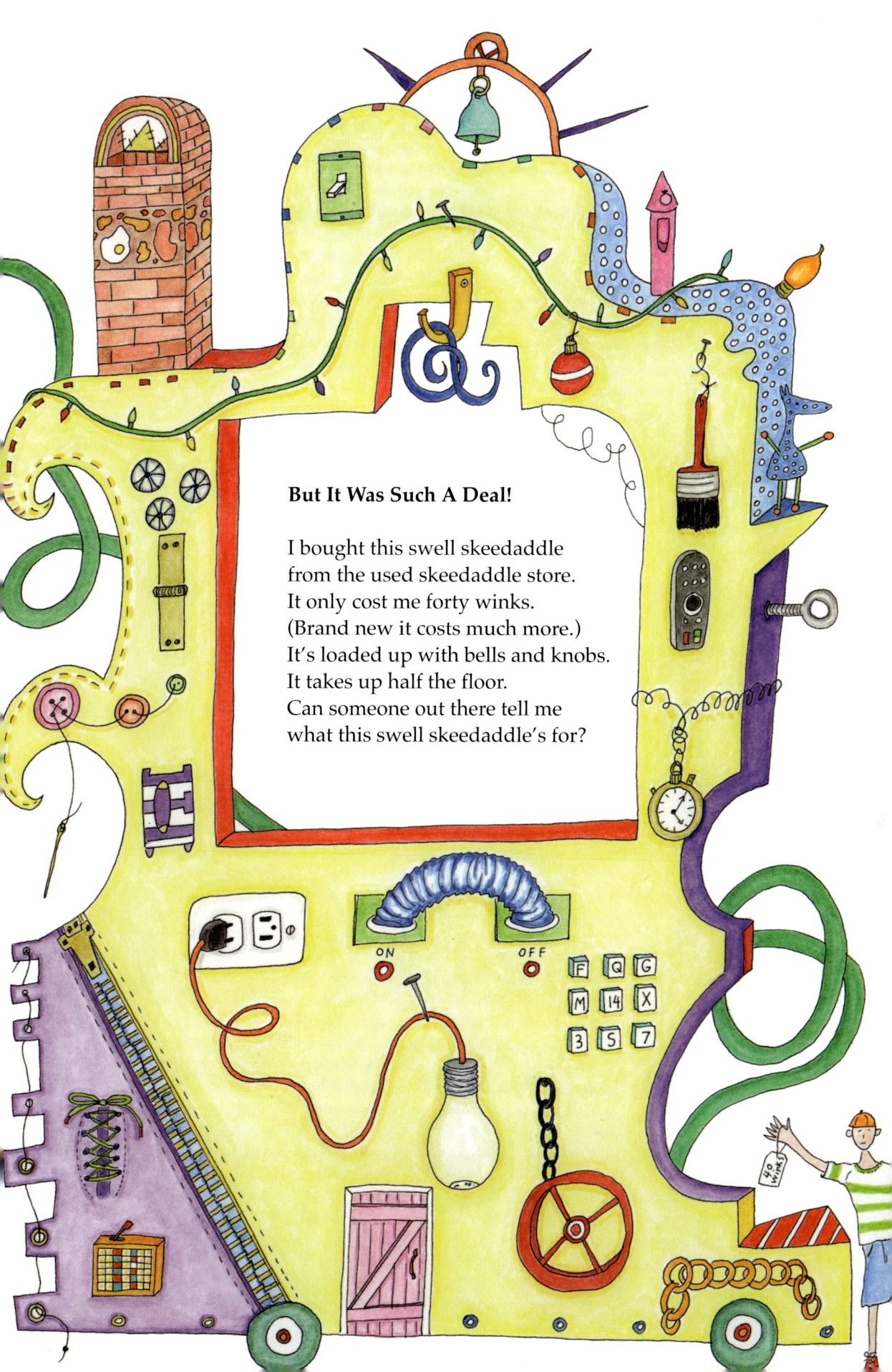

But It Was Such A Deal!

I bought this swell skeedaddle
from the used skeedaddle store.
It only cost me forty winks.
(Brand new it costs much more.)
It's loaded up with bells and knobs.
It takes up half the floor.
Can someone out there tell me
what this swell skeedaddle's for?

Shall We Meet Again at Lunch?

I do not think that I will eat
that monster coming down the street.

He's just a hundred times my size.
I'm betting he'd go good with fries.

Uh-oh. He's got me in his sights
and measuring me up in bites.

For him this street's one big buffet
of human, Ford, and Chevrolet.

But then he squints. I see him pause
(as buses crunch beneath his paws).

I think he recognizes me
and he might know my history

of eating far beyond my weight,
of cleaning every single plate,

of eating everything in sight,
of eating morning, noon, and night.

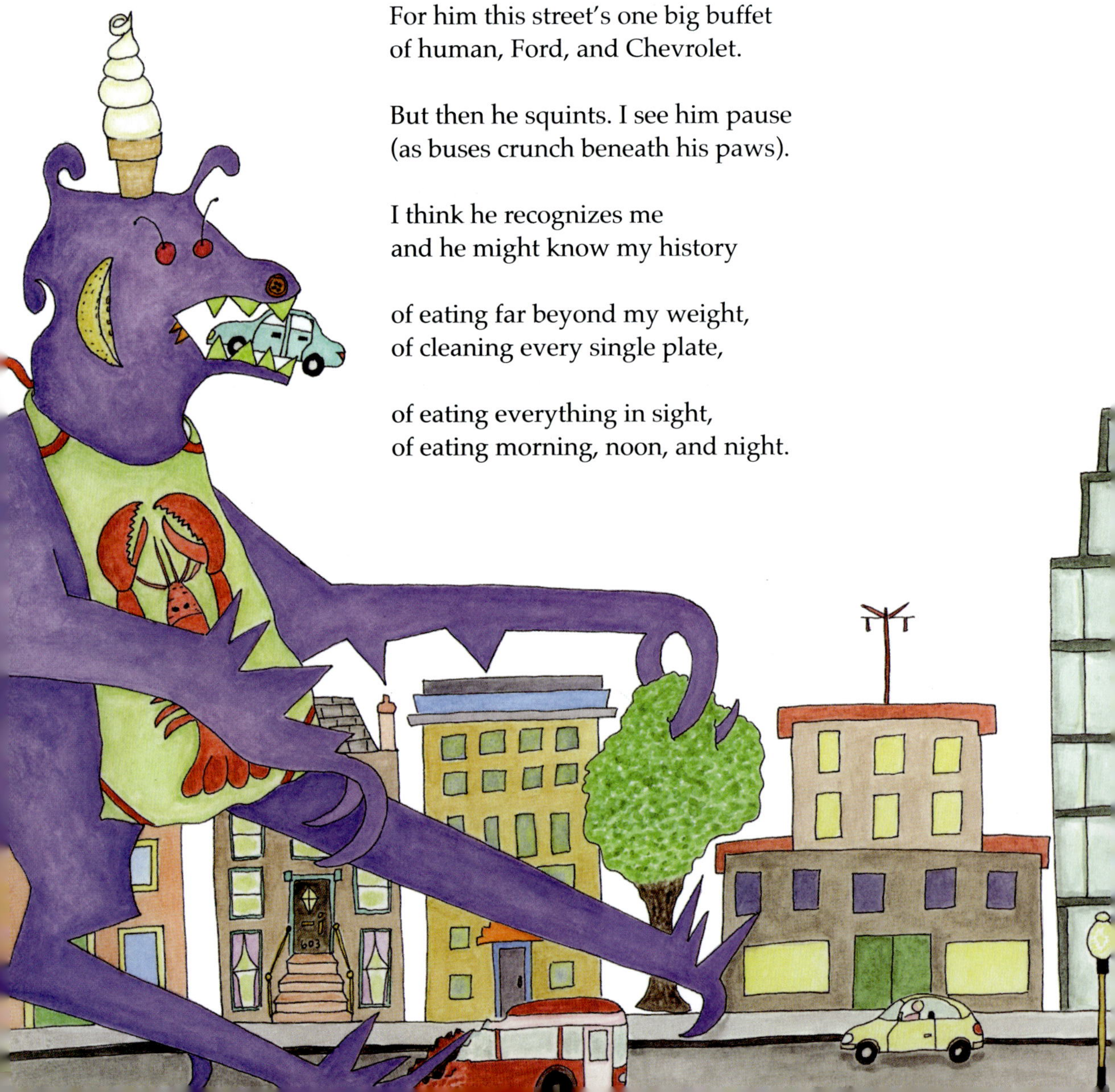

Oh sure, he's got a certain style
as he chomps lampposts by the mile.

But once in a humongous slurp
I ate twelve pies—and didn't burp.

I don't speak monster. I can't say,
"Today is just your lucky day.

I'm late for getting off to school.
I don't have time to gnaw and drool.

For now I'll have to let you pass—
But watch out when I'm out of class!"

Perhaps he read my hungry eye—
But he just waved as he crunched by.

And I waved back, as you'd expect—
a sign of omnivore respect.

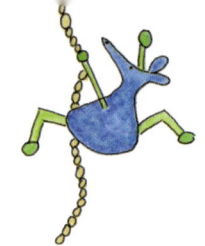

Anaconda Cargo

This company ships anything
from books to rocks to cats,
from railroad parts to works of art,
from cars to tools to hats.

And inside every box they ship
they put a special treat:
it is a gift ophidian
that hugs you on receipt.

Their packaging is guaranteed.
They've never had a theft.
They have a built-in guardian
with every package left.

When Grandma ships your birthday gift
to make sure you survive
you might not want to be there
when the underroos arrive.

I Prefer the Combo

Giant caterpillar.
Wing from dusty moth.
Shredded bits of snake-skin.
Worn and tattered cloth.
Strawberry peanut butter.
Brown and runny flan.
Hair of flying monkey.
Tuna from a can.
Alligator eyelids.
Knobs from camel's knees.
That's what I like on pizza.
But I'll settle for just cheese.

Brok the Thunderrer

My Name is Brok the Thunderrer.
My tale is widely known.
My appetite is legend
My muscles are like stone.

My Name is Brok the Thunderrer.
I have a hero's stride.
My legs are big as tree trunks.
I have a hairy hide.

My Name is Brok the Thunderrer.
I have a sword and shield.
My helmet is adorned with horns—
and I will never yield.

My Name is Brok the Thunderrer
and I am here to say
none of my royal retinue
must rise from bed today.

My Name is Brok the Thunderrer.
I have no need for school.
I should be out there plundering.
It is the savage rule.

My Name is Brok the Thunderrer.
Oh! Someone calls my name.
I fear it's Sis the Dragoness
whose very voice is flame.

My Name is Brok the Thunderrer.
I go to meet my doom.
My story ends with these few words:
HE HAD TO CLEAN HIS ROOM.

I've Lost My Blue Galoopa

I've lost my Blue Galoopa.
My Red one is alright.
But I must have two Galoopas
or I won't get through the night.

I've searched all through the garden.
I've searched all through the house.
I questioned every closet
and interviewed each mouse.

With just my Red Galoopa
I can almost guarantee
my alarm clock will stop ringing
or I might fall from a tree.

My books might topple over.
My shirt might come undone.
I might walk in a circle
or float into the sun.

So count your shoes and verify
your winter coat is on
'cause you don't know real trouble
'till your Blue Galoopa's gone.

My Plan for Success

I'll be on TV next week.
I hear that is the place
where a person gets attention
and reporters in their face.

Everyone will love me.
They won't care how I dress.
They won't care if my homework's done
or that my room's a mess.

Even if I skip my bath
my fame will be assured.
And if I'm understanding right
no one will say a word.

I'll be on TV next week,
relaxing just a smidge.
I think I finally got it right—
last week I was on fridge.

One Missing Ingredient

The lion, releasing me, said,
"Our picnic was totally spread.
We'd much rather chew
on a sandwich of YOU—
but we've gone and forgotten the bread!"

The Elephant

If he gets tickled
in his trunkular
his sneeze will knock you
perpendunkular.

Caveman Frozen in the Ice!

The missing link! Neanderthal!
Cro-Magnon! Man before the Fall!

A frozen man! We had to go
to see this cold museum show.

People dictate history
by seeing what they want to see.

The creature we saw frozen there
was really missing Auntie Claire.

You should have seen the look of dread
upon the face of Uncle Fred.

You'll understand how this is news:
he said he lost her on a cruise.

The scientists will laugh and scoff
but her dress should have tipped them off.

And if the light's exactly right
you'll see her wig's not on too tight.

A frozen caveman? We think not.
Our Auntie Claire is who they've got.

And if there's ever any doubt
we'll simply have to thaw her out.

Unfair Comparison

Young Hercules just turned his head
and found two snakes there in his bed.
He tied their tails into a knot
then tossed them from his baby cot.

If just one snake should cross my knees
would I be brave as Hercules?
I'm thinking I would run a lot.
That's why he's myth—and I am not.

Leading the Way

Surfing molten lava!
It's easy if you try.
I need a sturdy surfboard
that's not inclined to fry.
My toes cannot be hanging.
I dodge the ash and flame.
No one else is doing it.
I like the path to fame.

Swimming with Piranhas!
It's easy if you try.
I dive into their turgid pool.
I look them in the eye
I tell them I'll be swimming there.
Their nibbling must end!
No one else is doing it.
I like to set the trend.

Sleeping in the cactus!
It's easy if you try.
I simply find the greenish spots
that no quills occupy.
I wear my steel pajamas.
I grip my tweezers tight.
No one else is doing it.
I think I'm pretty bright.

My brothers pushed me forward.
"It's easy if you try.
Our baby sister's diaper stinks.
You're the lucky guy
who gets to change her. Here's a mask
and gloves and mop. Goodbye!"
No one else is doing it.
I'm comprehending why.

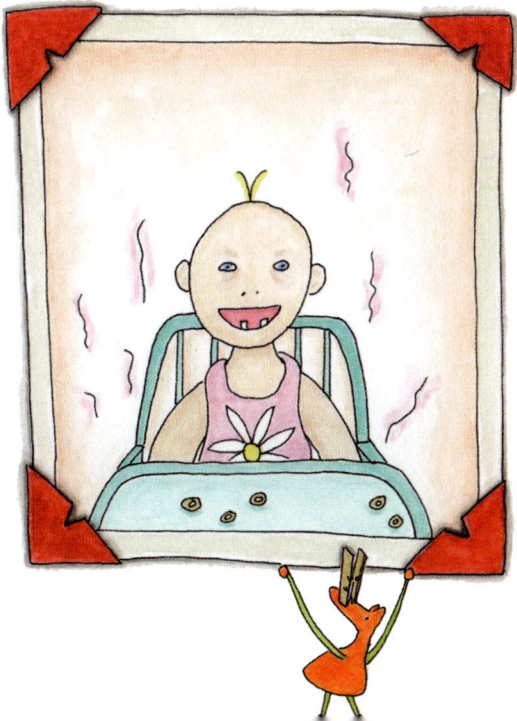

When Blob Jr. Went to Camp

When Blob Jr. spent six weeks
At Camp Mahooloowokkensqueeks
his Blob-folks worried by the phone.
He'd never been so long alone.

They'd bought him all the good scout stuff
so roughing it would not be rough:
Bandana, hat, a book on stars—
and bags of blobby candy bars.

The scouts there didn't raise a fuss
although he was gelatinous.
So what if he was shapeless goo?
He was another boy scout too!

He couldn't really push an oar
so he just blobbed there on the shore.
He had no hands for tying knots.
He oozed when he tried throwing pots.

His run was like a slimy crawl.
He couldn't throw a disc or ball.
There was no merit badge for 'Sit'.
He played a rock in their big skit.

But he could track and he could climb
and he had skills unique for slime.
For unformed pink phenomena
he hummed a stirring kum-ba-yah.

But his best skill was late at night
in shadows 'round the campfire light.
He'd keep the other scouts up late
with tales of kids his dad had ate.

Tom Pterodactyl

Flippity flappity.
Tom Pterodactyl
was scared of the
antediluvian nights.

Instead of just hiding
from all things Jurassic
he rode a big bicycle
covered with lights.

Medusa and Her Sister

Medusa had the mythic gift
of turning men to stone.
With this peculiar beauty skill
you'd think she lived alone.

The stories say that—but she had
a sister, if you please.
Her name was Gorgonzola—
and she turned all men to cheese.

And I mean really smelly cheese,
bad aromatic stuff,
all blue and pebbly and wrong,
where one whiff was enough.

Medusa had rock boyfriends
that were always there to stay.
But poor old Gorgonzola's
suitors drove the mice away.

Brave foolish men who dodged the awful
calcifying wink
might dare to choose the other girl
and wind up as a stink!

What did these girls do to the Gods
who gave them such a curse?
Sure, men to stone is pretty bad—
but men to cheese is worse.

Oh, one day you might catch a scent
of something pretty foul.
It might be socks, or moldy bread.
It makes your friends all scowl.

If folks around you scatter and there's
not a mouse in sight
it might be Gorgonzola
so keep your eyes shut tight.

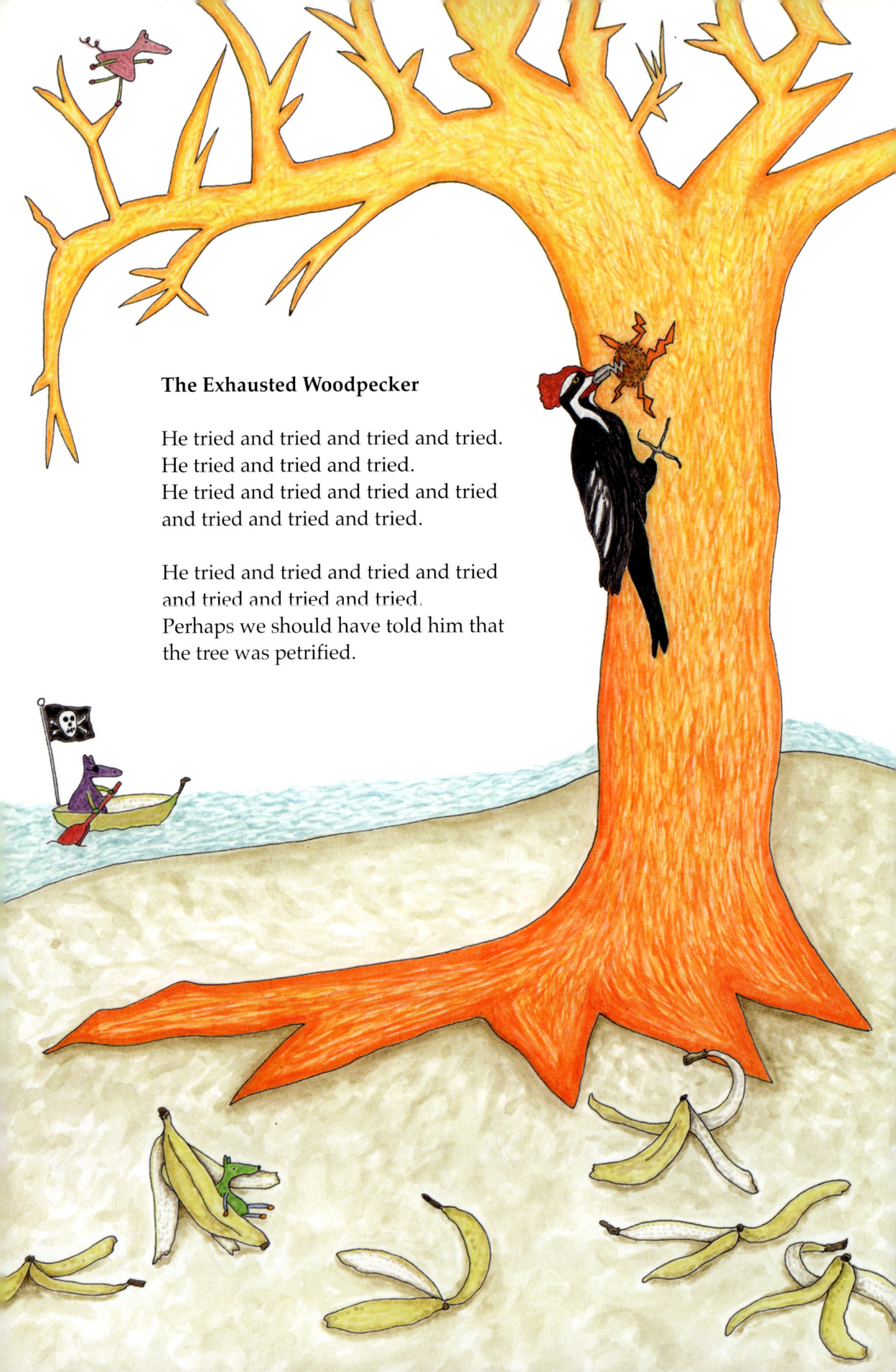

The Exhausted Woodpecker

He tried and tried and tried and tried.
He tried and tried and tried.
He tried and tried and tried and tried
and tried and tried and tried.

He tried and tried and tried and tried
and tried and tried and tried.
Perhaps we should have told him that
the tree was petrified.

Camping on Skull Island

I can handle the mosquitoes
that come as big as cars.
I don't mind the pterodactyls
whose wings blot out the stars.

Tyrannosaurs are fearsome—
burnt wienies calm their roars.
The giant spiders look mean—but—
they have a thing for s'mores.

But I like to eat bananas,
a bunch, or more, each day
So, I need some good repellent
to keep Giant Apes away!

Lizard Trouble

The gnu, the yak, the grizzly bear—
Write poems about them. They don't care.
Komodos, on the other hand,
are very clear on where they stand.

Don't write about them. Not a line.
It might be awful or divine.
If you should put them in a verse
they'll change your life from bad to worse.

Exactly how they learn that you
are writing sonnets or haiku
about their royal scaly-ness
they're in no hurry to confess.

Suffice to say they'll catch a plane.
They'll hail a taxi, board a train.
They'll find a way to your front door
and show you one mad dinosaur.

They'll eat your grass and chew your trees.
They'll try to gnaw your neighbor's knees.
They'll read your mail and claw your fence.
I'm speaking from experience.

So write your poems on spotted dogs,
chinchillas, millipedes, and hogs.
But leave your poems komodo-free
or you will end up just like me.

Potatoes Are Attacking

Potatoes are attacking.
They do it every night.
They sneak into the garden
and make the squash take flight.

They terrorize the turnips.
They beat up on the beans.
They taunt the jalapeños
and tease the mustard greens.

They give the melons wedgies.
They stomp the corn to cream.
They make tomatoes quiver
and make the carrots scream.

But shhh, don't go and tell them.
I'm here to make a stand
with a holster full of butter
and a masher in my hand!

Sleepover!

When Mummy boys stay overnight
They do the things young boys all should.
They take off all their Mummy wraps
And streak the neighborhood.

Sylvia Snorkleby

Sylvia Snorkleby liked to eat toast.
She liked it with thistles and gravel the most.
She liked it with ice cream or sheets from her bed.
She liked it with dogs doing tricks on her head.

She liked toast with cactus, she liked toast with cats.
She liked toasty sandwiches made with old bats
(which made the toast chewy and gave it a squeak—
she found they were best if they sat for a week.)

Her parents said, "Sylvia! Eat toast with jam!
Try it with marmalade, butter, or ham!
Or bacon or goose eggs, fritters or grits—
just something that won't give your tummy the fits!"

Said Sylvia Snorkleby, after a chew,
"That is what all of the normal kids do.
But my name is Snorkleby so I feel bound
to eat in a way that will shock and astound!"

Her parents puffed up with familial pride
while Sylvia gobbled on toast that was fried
in some type of sauce that was made from old snails
and small bits of garnish she trimmed from her nails.

Whatever strange things will upset you the most
then Sylvia Snorkleby's tried it on toast!
So my story's done. Here's my warning to you:
Be thankful your name isn't Snorkleby too!

Where the Dwermies Dwell

My mother always told the tale
of places where the Dwermies dwell
"…who'll snatch up children just like you
who don't do what they're told to do!

The Dwermies are an awful bunch.
They eat children's arms for lunch.
And for a snack, when meal is done,
they'll eat your fingers one by one.

Their arms are long and drag the ground.
Their eyes are big and red and round.
They lurk in caves and rotting trees,
in old boots, dead roots, 'neath your knees.

If you don't bathe for quite a spell
the Dwermies track you by your smell.
And don't go out at night alone
in case the Dwermies hear your bones.

If you don't like to go to bed,
if you don't like to wash the dishes,
if you don't like to take the trash,
if you don't like to feed your fishes,

if you don't like to go to school,
if when you're called you're always late,
if you don't do the jobs you're asked
I tell you what—you're Dwermie bait!

In case you think that you've been missed,
the Dwermies have you on their list.
That way if you do something rotten
then the deed won't be forgotten.

Now, say your prayers and go to sleep.
May all your dreams be sweet and deep.
If not and you refuse my warning…
Good night. I'll see you in the morning."

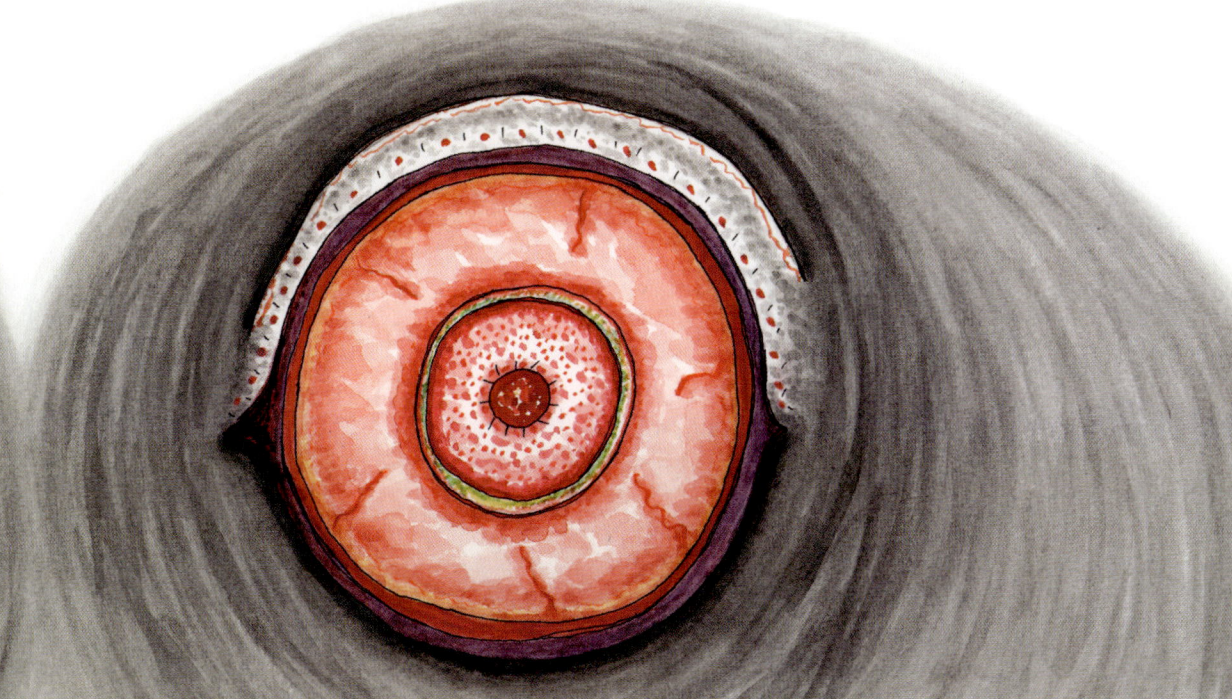

Finale

That's all there is.
It's time to go.
That's all the stories
that I know.
I've asked Mom
to turn out the light.
Goodbye, goodbye.
Goodnight, goodnight.

this
is
a
SMURgLet